The Eternal Frost

Written By Remington Keyes

Copyright © 2024 Remington Keyes
All rights reserved.

This Book is a work of fiction. Any similarity to actual persons, living or dead, or actual events, is purely coincidental.

This Book is dedicated to every reader who picks up this book and finds a piece of themselves within these chapters. Thank you for giving my words a chance.

Table of Contents

Chapter 1: New Beginnings

Two months had slipped by since Ravanna vanished into the shadows, leaving a void in the wake of her disappearance. For Deon, a teenager wielding the fiery essence of the universe, those months had been a turbulent whirlwind of chaos and revelation. It all began with a simple wish upon ancient gems, a wish that inadvertently thrust him into a battle against the malevolent forces seeking to misuse their power.

The Effects of the wish that was made had created a ripple effect that made the world feel different—quieter, somehow emptier. Ravanna was gone, her existence erased from the fabric of their friendship, leaving only the hollow echoes of what had been. The absence of her presence was a palpable void, an ache that seemed to resonate through every corner of their lives.

Deon's transformation into The Eternal Flame began soon after, a result of the immense power he had harnessed. His newfound abilities came with a responsibility that was both exhilarating and isolating. The weight of his powers and the expectations placed upon him created a distance between him and those he once held dear.

Booker, grappling with the loss of Ravanna and the changes in Deon, felt like a spectator in a world that had spun out of control. His own sense of self-worth was eroded by the growing divide between him and his best friend. The once-solid bond they shared now seemed fragile and strained, overshadowed by Deon's superhero persona and the unresolved grief that lingered in Booker's heart.

In the relentless struggle to safeguard the Galactic Gems, Deon found himself confronting a formidable adversary. Azazel, a being of unfathomable power, stood as a daunting obstacle between Deon and the peace he so fervently sought for his friends and his world. The clash was inevitable, the stakes immeasurable. And in a crescendo of raw power and sheer determination, Deon emerged victorious, shattering Azazel's hold and securing the safety of Earth.

With Azazel's defeat, tranquility washed over the planet once more, a soothing balm to the scars of conflict. Yet, amidst the jubilation of victory, Deon stood at the threshold of a new chapter in his life.

As the denizens of Earth reveled in the blissful ignorance of their savior's identity, Deon contemplated the weight of anonymity. The heroism that had preserved their existence remained shrouded, a silent guardian in the shadows. But peace, as fleeting as it was precious, brought with it complacency, a fertile ground for the seeds of villainy to take root once more.

"I see her in my thoughts every day," Deon mused, his voice a whisper against the backdrop of bustling streets. "If only she knew... But she can never know. I've chosen a path of solitude, a path she can never tread."

The sound of a car door opening shattered the stillness, drawing Deon's attention to the arrival of familiar faces. Booker, his steadfast companion since the days of innocence, stepped forth, accompanied by a new presence, Chad.

"Deon!" Booker's voice carried the warmth of camaraderie. "It's been too long."

"How's it going?" Deon's inquiry held a weight of its own, a reflection of the trials endured in the intervening months.

"I've been keeping busy," he replied, a hint of weariness underlying his words.

Introductions followed, unveiling Chad as Booker's new boyfriend. Pleasantries exchanged, Deon found himself caught in the ebb and flow of casual conversation, a semblance of normalcy in the wake of upheaval.

"I've heard much about you," Chad admitted, his tone tinged with a nervous energy.

The trio ventured into the bustling confines of the Woodland mall, the pulse of life echoing in the corridors of commerce. Yet, beneath the facade of ordinary existence, tensions simmered, unseen but palpable.

"I'll catch up with you guys in a bit," Chad announced, his departure a brief interlude in the rhythm of their day.

"He seems alright," Deon remarked, seeking solace in the familiar cadence of friendship.

"I just hope my parents will accept us," Booker confessed, a shadow of apprehension clouding his features.

"They will," Deon reassured, offering a beacon of optimism amidst uncertainty.

As they ventured deeper into the heart of the mall, a
    sanctuary of consumerism and distraction, Deon couldn't
    help but wonder what the future held. In a world
    teetering on the edge of chaos, where heroes and villains
    danced in the shadows, he knew one thing for certain:
The journey was far from over.

Booker wrapped his arm around Chad's waist as they
    strolled down the quiet streets of their neighborhood, the
    summer sun beginning to set behind the rows of houses.
    The air was warm, with a slight breeze that stirred the
    trees above them, rustling the leaves in a soothing
    whisper. It was a perfect evening, and Chad's laughter
    rang out, filling the space between them with a
    comforting joy that made Booker's heart swell.

"Are you sure you're okay with just hanging out tonight?"
    Chad asked, tilting his head to look at Booker, his blue
    eyes catching the last rays of sunlight. "I know you've
    been kind of stressed lately."

Booker smiled, though it didn't quite reach his eyes. "Yeah,
    I'm good. Besides, I could use a quiet night. It feels like
    everything's been moving so fast, you know?"

Chad nodded, leaning into Booker's side. "I get it. You've been through a lot with Deon and all that superhero stuff. It's gotta be tough seeing your best friend change like that."

"It is," Booker admitted, his voice soft. "But it's not just that. I feel…weird lately, like something's off." He hesitated, unsure how to put his feelings into words. How could he explain the strange chills he'd been feeling, or the way the air around him seemed to drop in temperature whenever he was upset? It sounded crazy, even to him.

Chad's expression grew concerned, and he stopped walking, turning to face Booker fully. "Weird how? Are you getting sick or something?"

Booker shook his head. "No, it's not that. It's more like…I don't know, like I'm different. Like there's something inside me that's trying to get out."

Chad studied him for a moment, then smiled reassuringly. "Well, whatever it is, we'll figure it out together. You're not in this alone, Booker."

The sincerity in Chad's words warmed Booker's heart, but there was still a lingering unease he couldn't shake. He opened his mouth to say more, but before he could, a sharp gust of wind swept down the street, chilling the air around them. Booker shivered, pulling Chad closer instinctively.

"Whoa, where did that come from?" Chad exclaimed, rubbing his arms. "It was warm just a second ago."

Booker frowned, looking around. The wind had come out of nowhere, sudden and unexplainable. He could feel the cold deep in his bones, a familiar sensation that had been happening more and more often lately. He didn't want to admit it, but a part of him knew this wasn't just a random gust of wind.

"Let's get home," Booker said, trying to shake off the feeling. "I don't like the way the air feels right now."

Chad nodded, and they quickened their pace, the warmth of their earlier stroll replaced by a growing sense of unease. Booker couldn't help but glance back over his shoulder as they walked, half-expecting to see something following them. But there was nothing there—just the shadows growing longer in the fading light.

Booker and Chad pulled up to Chad's house from the mall, in Booker's old car, the engine rumbling like an aged beast. Despite its worn appearance, it faithfully transported them to their destination. The two friends stepped out, the weight of their camaraderie evident in their easy banter.

As they reached Chad's house, Booker felt a sudden, sharp pain in his head, like a spike of ice driving through his skull. He stumbled, and Chad caught his arm, concern etched on his face.

"Booker, are you okay?"

Booker nodded, though his vision was swimming. "Yeah, I'm fine. Just a headache."

"Maybe you should come inside, lie down for a bit."

Booker wanted to protest, but the pain was too intense. He allowed Chad to lead him inside, where the warmth of the house enveloped him, a stark contrast to the cold still clinging to his skin. He sank onto the couch, clutching his head as the pain ebbed and flowed, like waves crashing against a shore of ice.

Inside Chad's house, they settled onto the couch, a haven of comfort after a long day's escapades.

"Let me get you some water," Chad said, hurrying to the kitchen.

As soon as Chad was out of sight, Booker felt the temperature in the room drop. He looked down at his hands, seeing frost forming on his fingertips, creeping across his skin like a living thing. Panic surged in his chest, and he clenched his fists, willing the frost to disappear. To his relief, it slowly melted away, leaving his hands trembling but normal once more.

Chad returned with a glass of water, and Booker quickly shoved his hands into his pockets, forcing a smile. "Thanks," he said, taking the glass with shaky fingers.

Chad sat down beside him, watching him closely. "Are you sure you're okay? You look really pale."

Booker nodded, sipping the water to avoid having to speak. His mind was racing, a thousand questions and fears tumbling over each other. What was happening to him? Was this connected to Deon's powers? And most importantly, how was he going to explain this to Chad?

The television flickered to life, casting a soft glow across the room as the news anchor's voice filled the space.

"The rest of The Cobra Cult escaped, but tonight The Cobra King remains under heavy surveillance. It was all thanks to the mysterious hero with flame powers," the anchor reported before Chad clicked the TV off with a roll of his eyes.

"What an ego on that guy," Chad remarked, prompting Booker to defend the hero.

"Hey, he can't help it if he's on fire with taking down crime," Booker quipped, reaching for the last slice of pizza.

But before he could claim it, Adrianna, Chad's sister, swooped in and snatched it away. "Uh-uh, don't you ever go home?" she teased, her playful scolding directed at Booker.

While Cuddling with a pillow on the couch, Booker retorted with a smirk, "Don't you have a man to bother?" he asked, earning a chuckle from Chad. Adrianna, unfazed, continued, "You smell stale pizza. You're here so much you should be paying our rent."

Chad jumped to Booker's defense, affectionately referring to him as "my man Booker," while Adrianna persisted, pointing out their constant presence at their home. "You two never hang at bookers house," she pointedly remarked, causing Chad to press Booker about his reluctance to invite him over.

Booker, initially dismissive, found himself on the defensive. "Well, what about the time that, uh... or remember the time we, uh..." His attempts at diversion fell flat as Chad confronted him about their three-month-long relationship and the absence of any invitation to meet Booker's family.

Caught off guard, Booker stumbled over his words. "I'm more comfortable over here, that's all. Why are you nagging me over this?" he countered, attempting to deflect Chad's inquiries.

Chad persisted, expressing a desire for a change of pace. "I'm not," Booker protested weakly, realizing the weight of Chad's request. "We just need a little change of pace," Chad repeated, his tone gentle yet firm.

Relenting, Booker reluctantly agreed to have Chad over, though his reluctance lingered. "I guess I understand," he conceded, committing to a Sunday night visit. But as Chad pressed for specifics, Booker's evasion became apparent.

"How soon?" Chad prodded, sensing Booker's hesitation.

"Uh... this Sunday night?" Booker offered, his uncertainty palpable.

Chad accepted the invitation, though his skepticism remained. "You sure?" he pressed, prompting Booker to reaffirm his commitment with forced enthusiasm.

"Yeah, yeah, that will work," Booker assured him, mentally preparing himself for the impending visit. "Sunday it is then," Chad declared, sealing the arrangement with a finality that left Booker with no room for escape.

As Chad laid out his expectations for the evening, Booker couldn't shake the feeling of apprehension that settled in the pit of his stomach. "Better tell your parents to stock up on essentials. Netflix, chips, sodas. The basics," Chad advised, unknowingly adding to Booker's mounting anxiety.

With the agreement made and plans in motion, Booker couldn't help but wonder how he would navigate the impending introduction of his two worlds—his home and his sanctuary at Chad's house.

Within the dimly lit confines of the Cobra Cult's new hideout, tension hung thick in the air like a suffocating fog. Jim Murray, the formidable leader of the notorious gang, stood seething with rage. His fists clenched, he unleashed a powerful blow upon the unsuspecting wall, the sound echoing through the cavernous space.

"That super powered freak put Cobra on lockdown," Murray growled, his voice laced with venomous anger.

Hal Kent, a loyal member of the gang, nodded in agreement, though his eyes betrayed a hint of fear. "Yeah, he's always causing trouble," he muttered cautiously.

With a sudden surge of fury, Murray seized Kent by the collar, his fingers tightening around the fabric of his leather jacket with a vice-like grip. "He can't keep busting our business and bringing us down," he spat, his eyes burning with intensity. "We need a superpower thug of our own. Playtime is over."

Struggling to regain his composure under Murray's menacing glare, Kent managed a feeble attempt at humor. "Geez, a boss with an attitude," he quipped, the sarcasm evident in his tone.

But Murray's expression remained unyielding, his determination etched into every line of his face. In the shadows of their clandestine lair, a sinister plan began to take shape, as the Cobra Cult prepared to strike back with a ferocity born of desperation.

Chapter 2: The Early Days Together

In the warm glow of the summer sun, the small town of Woodland, Massachusetts seemed to hold infinite possibilities for young Deon and Booker. The two had been inseparable since their early days at the local playground, their laughter echoing through the streets as they crafted adventures out of mundane objects. Their friendship was a tapestry woven from countless shared moments, each thread a testament to their bond.

Booker had always admired Deon's effortless charm and boundless confidence. Deon, in turn, appreciated Booker's unwavering loyalty and quiet strength. They were two halves of a whole, navigating the world with a camaraderie that seemed to defy the very fabric of fate. Together, they tackled every challenge with a sense of invincibility that only childhood could bestow.

It was during these formative years that Ravanna entered their lives, weaving her own vibrant threads into their friendship. She was a force of nature, a whirlwind of passion and defiance that captivated Deon's heart. The trio became a steadfast unit, their adventures expanding beyond the confines of the playground to the realms of their imagination.

Ravanna's presence was a spark that ignited Deon's creativity and determination. She challenged him in ways he hadn't anticipated, pushing him to confront his own fears and aspirations. For Booker, it was a joy to witness Deon's burgeoning love for Ravanna, even as he occasionally felt like a third wheel in their blossoming relationship.

As The Eternal Flame, Deon became a symbol of hope and power, his fiery abilities a beacon in the darkness. His heroic deeds were celebrated, and his every move was scrutinized by the public. The contrast between Deon's heroic persona and Booker's everyday existence became increasingly stark.

Booker observed the changes from the sidelines, his feelings of inadequacy and isolation deepening. Deon's superhero status brought him admiration and adoration, but it also drew him away from his old life. The bond that had once been the cornerstone of their friendship now seemed overshadowed by the demands of Deon's new role.

The superhero's busy schedule, public appearances, and constant battles left little room for the mundane moments that had once defined their friendship. Booker found himself grappling with the sense that he was no longer an integral part of Deon's life, and the feeling of being left behind gnawed at him.

The chasm between Booker and Deon grew wider with each passing day. Booker's own struggles were compounded by the sense that he would never measure up to the extraordinary life Deon had embraced. He wrestled with feelings of insecurity, questioning his own worth and wondering if he would ever be special in his own right.

Booker's attempts to carve out his own path were often overshadowed by the grandeur of Deon's superhero exploits. He felt like a shadow in the wake of The Eternal Flame, his own achievements seeming insignificant in comparison. The fear of never being able to match Deon's greatness became a pervasive thought, affecting every aspect of Booker's life.

The strain on their friendship became more apparent as time went on. Misunderstandings and unspoken grievances festered, creating a rift that seemed insurmountable. Booker's jealousy and frustration were often misinterpreted by Deon, who was too preoccupied with his responsibilities to fully grasp the depth of his friend's struggles.

Booker's attempts to bridge the gap were met with frustration and confusion. The moments they once shared, filled with laughter and camaraderie, were now replaced by awkward silences and tense conversations. The connection that had once been a source of strength was now a source of pain, and both struggled to navigate the shifting dynamics of their relationship.

Chapter 3: Embracing Identity

Booker's room was a treasure trove of wonders, at least to Chad's eyes.

"Wow, all this stuff is so cool," Chad exclaimed.

Booker, with an air of expected pride, responded, "But, of course."

"And you said meeting your parents would be a snore fest... So it's only three for dinner, huh?" Chad inquired.

"What can I say, my dad's working," Booker explained.

As Bookers Mom entered the room, she greeted Chad warmly, "Hi, Chad. It's nice to meet you. Boys, it's time for dinner. Make sure to wash up."

Chad commented on the inviting smell, to which Bookers Mom graciously replied, "Thank you, Chad."

Seated around the dinner table, Booker mustered the courage to broach a delicate subject with his mother, "Mom, I'd like to talk to you. Chad is here because he's my friend."

With a knowing expression, Bookers Mom nodded, "Mm-hmm."

"My boyfriend. Because… I'm gay. I hope you can accept me," Booker confessed nervously.

Bookers Mom's reaction was unexpected, "Whoa! Hold your horses, son. I already knew you were gay."

"You did?" Booker was taken aback.

"I'm your mother. I know who you are, Booker. Your father might need more time to wrap his head around this though," she reassured him.

"I don't know, I—" Booker started.

"It's okay, son, we'll figure this out," Bookers Mom interrupted as the door slammed in the background, announcing Bookers Dad's arrival.

"I think that's your father, I better go talk with him," Bookers Mom excused herself.

As they waited for Bookers Mom to return, Chad remarked, "I think that went well. I think it's cool that I get to meet your pops after all."

Booker cautioned, "It's not over yet..."

Todd, Booker's dad, barged in, clearly agitated, "On top of all that, traffic sucked. This city, Angela, this city…"

Chad greeted Todd politely, "Hey, Mr. Todd. Good to finally meet you."

Booker introduced Chad again, "Hey dad! This is my friend Chad, remember, I told you about him?"

"Not nearly enough," Todd grumbled.

Booker, feeling the need to explain, glanced at Chad and remarked, "He's not like this normally."

Chad tried to lighten the mood, "Hey, I've had bad days like that myself."

The dinner proceeded in silence until Chad broke it by clearing his throat, signaling a new opportunity for conversation. The dinner table atmosphere shifted as Chad attempted to steer the conversation toward a more positive topic.

"Booker, I brought over the new flyer for Pride Fest," Chad announced optimistically.

Booker responded with a promise, "I'll look at it after dinner. Then we can bake cookies."

However, Todd's reaction was anything but supportive. With a forceful slam of his fist on the table, he declared, "There will be no baking from any MAN in this house."

Bookers Mom intervened, her tone tinged with disgust, "Todd, please."

Ignoring her, Todd continued, revealing his outdated beliefs, "Angela, maybe I'm old-fashioned, but I don't think two boys should be 'baking' together."

Chad attempted to defend their activity, "Cooking is a positive outlet, Mr. Todd. It's very fun too."

Todd's response reflected his narrow-minded perspective, "He should be making cookies with a woman. Y'all want to tear any last manhood, guys like me, work hard to keep established. Look around me, rainbows and 'Little Pony's' everywhere, well not in my house…"

Booker tried to reason with his father, "Well dad, that's not fair."

But Todd shut down any further discussion with a final decree, "That's the last word, Booker."

As the echoes of dinner faded into the quiet hum of the evening, Booker and Chad sought solace in the familiarity of the living room. Yet, beneath the veneer of comfort, a storm brewed within Booker's troubled mind.

Pacing back and forth, Booker's voice trembled with embarrassment as he confided in Chad, "My dad... sometimes, y'know? I'm so embarrassed."

Chad, ever the voice of reason, attempted to quell Booker's unease, "Will you stop? My dad hates cooking too. It's an old-fashioned thing, not a ignorance thing. As far as I'm concerned, this whole thing is behind us."

Their fragile tranquility was shattered by the distant rumble of voices from upstairs, like thunder heralding an impending storm. Booker's parents, unaware of the ears that strained to catch their words, engaged in a heated exchange.

Todd's voice, thick with disapproval, carried down the staircase, "…and now I see why Booker acts like such a pussy, Ang. That kid's a bad influence. All people like him are. He's going to turn our kid into a fruit. It's bad enough I have to deal with them ruining my TV Shows; now one of them is in my home where I sleep."

In the wake of Todd's harsh words, Angela's gentle admission pierced the tension like a dagger, "Todd, our son is gay. That's what he was trying to tell you."

"I won't have a fruit living under my roof!" Todd said with disgust.

As the words of Booker's father echoed in the room, Chad's heart sank. He couldn't bear to stay any longer, the weight of those words pressing down on him.

"I... I gotta... I gotta go," Chad muttered, his voice heavy with emotion.

Booker's plea halted him in his tracks. "Chad, don't go. Please?"

Despite Booker's plea, Chad felt the urge to escape. "It's still early. I can call my pops for a ride," he offered weakly.

Desperation laced Booker's voice as he suggested an alternative. "We can talk to my mom."

Chad's response was tinged with bitterness. "What's that going to do? She can't change what he said. You were right all along, coming here was a bad idea." With that, he slammed the door shut, his anger palpable in the echoing sound.

Todd starts shouting down stairs. "Whats going on down there? All of a sudden the fairy can slam a door?" he says angrily.

Booker turns to his dad, with an angry facial expression, and says "Well you got what you wanted dad, My boyfriend is gone because of you and your stupid bigotry. I hate you!"

Todd yells from the top of the stairs, "I know you're not talking to me that way, boy, and thats with a small B. Don't you ever talk back to me. Alright? Because you're going to find yourself homeless, real quick." he says as he runs down the stairs. "Matter of fact, Get out! Get out! Get the hell outta my house! If you're gay, you don't get to live here anymore. Get out! Get out! You don't have that choice no more. Get outta my house before I run you out of my house."

Booker stood on the doorstep of his childhood home, his heart pounding with fear and uncertainty. The words of his Dad still echoed in his mind, sharp and painful. "I won't have a fruit living under my roof!"

With a heavy heart, Booker gathered his few belongings and stepped out into the cold night. He didn't know where he would go or what he would do. Tears stung his eyes as he walked aimlessly, the weight of rejection settling heavily on his shoulders.

As he wandered through the deserted streets, Booker felt a strange sensation coursing through him. It started as a tingling in his fingertips, then spread throughout his entire body. He looked down in confusion, only to see a thin layer of frost forming on the ground beneath his feet.

Panicked, Booker tried to shake off the icy feeling, but it only seemed to grow stronger. With each step he took, the frost spread further, coating everything in its path with a shimmering layer of ice.

Desperate for answers, Booker stumbled into an alleyway, away from prying eyes. He closed his eyes, trying to calm his racing thoughts. And then it happened.

With a surge of energy, Booker felt something inside him shift. It was as if a dam had burst, releasing a power he never knew he had. Ice erupted from his fingertips, swirling and dancing in the air around him.

Booker gasped in awe, watching as his newfound abilities took shape before his eyes. He could hardly believe it. He, Booker, had the power to control ice.

But as the initial rush of excitement faded, a wave of uncertainty washed over him. What did this mean for his future? How could he possibly navigate this new reality on his own?

The Next Morning, Booker trudged through the school gates, his backpack slung over his shoulder and a heavy weight in his chest. The events of the previous night still weighed heavily on his mind as he navigated the familiar halls of his high school, now feeling like a stranger in his own world.

He had spent a restless night in an alleyway, the bitter cold seeping into his bones as he struggled to come to terms with his newfound reality. And now, as he faced the prospect of another day at school, his anxiety threatened to consume him.

As Booker entered the classroom, he felt a sense of unease wash over him. He knew that he couldn't afford to let his guard down, not with his powers still so unpredictable. But he couldn't shake the feeling of dread that lingered in the pit of his stomach.

Deon noticed the tension in Booker's demeanor and offered him a reassuring smile, but even that couldn't dispel the cloud of worry that hung over them both.

Booker couldn't resist the urge to show Deon his new abilities. With a flick of his wrist, he conjured a delicate snowflake, watching in amazement as it danced through the air before melting away into nothingness.

Deon's eyes widened in wonder, a smile spreading across his face. "That's incredible, Booker! You have to show me more."

But before Booker could respond, the door to the classroom swung open, and Principal Maynard stepped inside, his expression stern and unwavering.

"What's going on here?" he demanded, his eyes narrowing as they landed on Booker.

Caught off guard, Booker stumbled over his words, struggling to explain himself. But before he could form a coherent response, Principal Maynard's gaze flickered to the remnants of snow on the ground, his expression darkening with concern.

"I should have known it was you," he said, his voice cold and accusatory. "Using your powers in school? You could injure somebody."

Booker's heart sank as he realized the gravity of the situation. He had hoped to keep his abilities a secret, at least until he could learn to control them. But now, it seemed that his secret was out, and there was no going back.

Principal Maynard's words echoed in Booker's ears as he watched helplessly, his heart heavy with regret. And as the reality of his actions sank in, he knew that his life would never be the same again.

The brisk wind danced through the trees outside Booker's former home, a stark contrast to the heaviness weighing down the atmosphere inside. Booker slumped into a chair at the kitchen table, his expression crestfallen. Angela, his mother, sat opposite him, her eyes filled with concern.

Booker fidgeted with his hands, his mind swirling with a whirlwind of emotions. After being kicked out of school for inadvertently revealing his newfound ice powers, he felt like his world was crumbling around him. But amidst the chaos, one thought gnawed at him more than any other: the acceptance of his true self.

"Mom," Booker began tentatively, his voice barely above a whisper, "I don't understand. How can someone as kind-hearted and open-minded as you can be married to someone who's... against having a gay son?"

Angela's gaze softened, her heart aching for her son's turmoil. She reached across the table, gently clasping Booker's trembling hands in hers. "Oh, sweetie," she sighed, "there's no logic to homophobia. It's born out of fear, ignorance, and sometimes, sadly, even hatred. But what's important is that you've made up your own mind, you know who you are, and you're happy with that."

Tears welled up in Booker's eyes as he absorbed his mother's words. Despite the storm raging outside and the turmoil within, her unwavering love and support offered him solace like a beacon in the night.

"But, Mom," Booker sniffled, his voice catching in his throat, "what if Dad never comes around? What if he never accepts me for who I am?"

Angela squeezed Booker's hands reassuringly, her gaze unwavering. "We can't control how others feel or react, Booker. But what we can control is how we choose to live our lives. And I choose to stand by him, 'till death due us part."

With a deep breath, Booker wiped away his tears, his resolve firming like ice thawing under the warmth of the sun. As the wind continued to howl outside, Angela and Booker sat in quiet solidarity, their hearts intertwined in a bond stronger than any adversity.

Chapter 4: The Cobra Strikes

As he stepped out, onto the damp streets of Woodland, they echoed with the distant rumble of thunder as Booker dashed through the alleyways, his heart pounding like a drum in his chest. He had narrowly escaped the clutches of some thugs thanks to his newfound ice powers, but he knew he couldn't let his guard down just yet.

Unbeknownst to him, a shadowy figure lurked in the darkness, observing his every move. It was a member of the notorious gang known as The Cobra Cult, their emblem emblazoned on his leather jacket like a badge of honor. As Booker disappeared into the night, the gang member's eyes gleamed with recognition - here was someone with powers beyond the ordinary.

Quickly, the gang member relayed the information to his comrades, and before long, Booker found himself cornered, surrounded by the menacing figures of The Cobra Cult. They dragged him away to their hideout, a derelict building tucked away in the heart of the city.

Locked in a dark room, Booker's mind raced with fear and uncertainty. What did these people want with him? And how did they know about his powers? The answers came swiftly as the gang's leader, Hal Kent, stepped into the room, a twisted smile playing on his lips.

"We know what you can do, Booker," Hal sneered, his voice dripping with malice. "And we're going to put those powers to good use."

Booker's heart sank as he realized the gravity of his situation. The Cobra Cult intended to use him as a pawn in their twisted games, holding him hostage until he agreed to do their bidding. But Booker was determined not to give in without a fight.

"I don't know what you're talking about," he replied, his voice trembling with defiance. "I don't have any powers."

Hal's laughter echoed off the walls, mocking and cruel. "Don't play dumb with me, kid. We saw what you did out there. Now tell us how it works, and maybe we'll let you live."

But Booker refused to yield. He kept his secret close to his chest, pretending ignorance even as his mind raced with possibilities. And then, in a moment of inspiration, he found a way to turn the tables.

As Hal advanced menacingly, Booker concentrated with all his might, summoning the power of ice to his fingertips. With a flick of his wrist, he froze the air around him, shaping it into a razor-sharp knife of solid ice.

Caught off guard, Hal stumbled backward, his eyes widening in shock. But before he could react, Booker broke free from his restraints and made a run for it, his frozen blade gleaming in the dim light.

Outside, the rain began to fall in earnest, the droplets mingling with the tears on Booker's cheeks as he faced off against The Cobra Cult. He knew he couldn't take them all on alone, but he refused to back down.

With each step, he felt the power of the storm coursing through his veins, lending him strength and resolve. And when one of the thugs gained the upper hand, Booker seized the opportunity, freezing a puddle beneath his feet and sending him crashing to the ground.

In the end, it was a battle fought with ice and rain, a clash of elements against a backdrop of darkness and despair. But against all odds, Booker emerged victorious, his adversaries scattered like leaves in the wind.

As he stood amidst the wreckage, Booker felt a surge of triumph unlike anything he had ever known. But as he turned to leave, his heart heavy with sorrow, he knew that his journey was far from over.

For out there, in the vast expanse of the city, countless dangers awaited him, lurking in the shadows like hungry wolves. But whatever challenges lay ahead, Booker was ready to face them head-on, armed with nothing but his courage and his newfound powers.

And so, with one last glance back at the scene of his victory, Booker disappeared into the night, his footsteps echoing faintly in the rain-soaked streets of Woodland.

The summer had been one of unexpected twists and turns for Deon. From battling against elemental adversaries to standing as a beacon of hope for Woodland, Massachusetts, he had embraced his role as a guardian with unwavering determination. As the season drew to a close, the town's gratitude washed over him like a warm embrace.

Labor Day arrived, and Chad's annual party was the highlight of the neighborhood's festivities. Deon, however, found himself running a bit behind schedule. Despite the allure of relaxation and celebration, duty always called to him. With a quick glance at the time, he hurried towards Chad's house, eager to join in the merriment.

Arriving slightly later than anticipated, Deon took in the scene with a smile. Laughter filled the air, mingling with the scent of barbecue and the chatter of friends. But before he could fully immerse himself in the festivities, his phone buzzed insistently in his pocket.

Curious, Deon answered the call, only to hear Booker's voice on the other end. The tension in Booker's tone was palpable as he asked to speak with Deon privately. Sensing the urgency, Deon hesitated for a moment before declining, citing more pressing matters at hand.

As he ended the call, Deon's gaze swept over the party, his mind still lingering on Booker's cryptic request. But before he could dwell on it further, chaos erupted. The lights flickered and then plunged the entire block into darkness. Murmurs of confusion filled the air as partygoers fumbled in the sudden gloom.

Without hesitation, Deon sprang into action. Drawing upon his innate power, he summoned flames to his fingertips, illuminating the darkness with a warm, golden glow. The room erupted into cheers as Deon's fire cast shadows dancing across the walls, banishing the darkness that had descended upon them.

As the party resumed in the newfound light, Deon couldn't shake the feeling of unease gnawing at him. Retrieving his phone from his pocket, he quickly scrolled through his social media feed, his heart sinking as he came across a post detailing the knockout of the local power station.

Realization dawned on him like a thunderclap. Booker's call, the sudden power outage—it was all connected. But why would Booker reach out to him, only to sabotage the power supply?

With determination hardening his resolve, Deon knew that his duty as a guardian extended beyond physical threats. It was his responsibility to protect the town from all dangers, no matter where they lurked. And as he surveyed the faces around him, bathed in the warm glow of his flames, he silently vowed to uncover the truth behind the shadows that threatened to engulf Woodland once more.

Deon raced through the streets, the urgency of the situation propelling him forward. As he approached the power station, a sense of dread washed over him. The building was enveloped in a thick layer of ice, shimmering in the pale moonlight.

With a deep breath, Deon focused his energy, summoning the flames within him. Heat radiated from his palms as he approached the icy barrier. With a swift motion, he unleashed a burst of fire, melting the frost and revealing the entrance to the power station.

But before he could enter, he felt a sudden chill in the air. Instinctively, he turned, just in time to see a figure emerge from the shadows. It was Booker, his old friend turned bitter rival. Ice crackled around Booker's hands as he formed snowballs, his expression twisted with hostility.

"Booker," Deon called out, his voice tinged with concern. "What are you doing here?"

Booker's response was immediate and aggressive. Without a word, he launched a barrage of snowballs at Deon, each one aimed with precision. Deon barely had time to react, his flames flickering as he tried to deflect the icy projectiles.

"Stop this, Booker!" Deon shouted, desperation creeping into his voice.

But Booker remained silent, his attacks relentless. Deon knew he had to end this confrontation before it escalated further. With a determined expression, he focused his energy, summoning a wall of flames to shield himself from Booker's onslaught.

"Show yourself, Booker!" Deon called out, his voice echoing in the frigid air. "This won't solve anything!"

For a moment, there was silence. Deon held his breath, waiting for a response. But instead of facing him head-on, Booker chose to retreat, disappearing into the darkness without a word.

Frustration boiled within Deon as he watched Booker slip away. He had hoped for answers, for resolution, but all he found was more questions. With a heavy heart, he extinguished the flames around him, the cold reality of the situation settling in.

As he stood outside the power station, Deon couldn't shake the feeling of unease. Whatever was happening, it was far from over. With determination in his heart, he vowed to uncover the truth, no matter where it led him. For Deon knew that the clash of elements was far from finished.

Chapter 5:
The Lost Child

The bustling Woodland mall was alive with the hum of shoppers and the chatter of voices echoing off polished floors. Deon strolled alongside his new friend from school, Lillian, their laughter blending with the ambient noise as they browsed through the stores. But as they turned a corner, Deon's jovial demeanor faltered when he spotted Booker across the bustling concourse.

Nearby, frost began to form on the windows, a telltale sign of Booker's presence. With a murmured apology, Deon excused himself from Lillian's side, his senses alert to the brewing tension.

Meanwhile, Booker, lost in admiration of a display of sparkling jewelry, found himself abruptly accosted by the storekeeper. Accusations of theft hung heavy in the air, fueled by the color of his skin. Anger surged within

Booker as he struggled against the unjust accusation, his newfound powers thrumming beneath his skin.

In a fit of rage and despair, Booker unleashed his icy abilities, coating the store in a sheen of frost and snow. Panic rippled through the crowd as chaos erupted, and Deon's heart clenched with dread as he heard the commotion.

With flames flickering to life at his fingertips, Deon dashed towards the source of the disturbance. His fiery aura illuminated the chaos as he struggled to contain the spreading frost, shielding innocent bystanders from harm.

But as he battled against the rising tide of ice, Deon found himself trapped beneath a towering pillar of frozen debris, his movements hindered by the weight of his own powers.

Amidst the chaos, Booker's gaze fell upon a young boy, huddled close to his mother in fear. Memories of his own childhood resurfaced, raw and painful, as he saw his past reflected in the frightened child's eyes.

Overwhelmed by guilt and remorse, Booker's resolve shattered, tears mingling with the frost on his cheeks as he fled the scene, leaving behind a trail of destruction in his wake.

By the time Deon managed to free himself from the icy prison, Booker had vanished into the maze of the mall, leaving behind a shattered storefront and a lingering sense of unease.

As Booker ventured through the winding trails of the nearby woods, an icy path trailed behind him, evidence of his uncontrollable ice powers. He found himself lost, his intended destination, Route 29 leading to Springfield, seemingly out of reach. It was then that he stumbled upon an old man, a chance encounter that would alter the course of his day.

"You seem to be lost. Do you need directions?" the old man inquired, his voice weathered but kind.

Booker glanced at his navigation app before replying, "The App says Route 29 leads to Springfield. Does this trail take me there?"

The old man nodded sagely. "According to my map, it does. Just be careful."

Determined to continue his journey, Booker pressed on. But his progress was halted by the sight of a shadowy figure ahead. "Huh?" he murmured, calling the old man's attention to the scene.

"It looks like some kind of kid?" the old man observed.

Booker approached cautiously and confirmed the old man's observation. The child, named Richie, seemed to be in distress, his small form trembling with fear and uncertainty.

"Hey Old Man!" Booker called out, concern lacing his voice. "The kid looks like he's in bad shape…"

As they debated whether the child needed medical attention, Richie's stubborn demeanor became evident as he rebuffed Booker's attempts to help. Despite their concern, they ultimately decided to leave the child be, trusting that his own father would soon return for him.

"I hope his parents come back soon," Booker remarked, a tinge of worry in his tone as they walked away, leaving Richie behind.

Their journey took an unexpected turn when they sought refuge from an impending storm in a nearby hospital. As they warmed themselves by the fireplace, thoughts of Richie lingered in Booker's mind.

"I wonder if anybody picked up that child yet? What if his parents just left him there?" Booker mused, his brow furrowed with concern.

The old man offered reassurance, but Booker couldn't shake the feeling of unease. His suspicions were confirmed when snippets of conversation from a group of thugs revealed the truth behind Richie's abandonment.

"He's the one that abandoned that kid," Booker declared with disgust, his gaze fixed on the callous individual responsible for Richie's plight.

Determined to right the wrong, Booker confronted the man, his resolve unwavering in the face of danger. But before the situation could escalate further, the intervention of two nurses diffused the tension, reminding them of their duty to help those in need.

Realizing the urgency of the situation, Booker and the old man raced against time to rescue Richie from the elements. Their efforts were met with unexpected challenges as they encountered a flock of vultures threatening the helpless child.

"Knock it off!" Booker commanded, his icy powers unleashed to fend off the attackers.

With Richie's safety secured, they rushed back to the hospital, their hearts pounding with the weight of their mission. As they burst through the doors, seeking aid for the ailing child, Nurse Dianna's expression mirrored their own concern.

"It's an emergency!" Booker exclaimed, urgency lacing his words as they pleaded for assistance.

With time running out, they could only hope that their efforts would be enough to save the lost child who had unwittingly crossed their path.

The waiting room was a symphony of hushed tones and anxious glances, each heartbeat marked by the ticking of the clock on the wall. The old man's voice broke through the heavy silence, laden with worry.

"Will he survive?" he asked, his eyes fixed on Nurse Dianna, who stood before him with a somber expression.

"Richie is very weak. How could you let him get into this condition?" Nurse Dianna's voice was gentle but tinged with a hint of reproach.

Booker, his features drawn tight with tension, stepped forward. "You can't blame us, we just saved him from dying."

The old man nodded in agreement. "Booker is right, it's not our fault. That jerk over there was the one who abandoned him."

Nurse Dianna's brows furrowed in confusion. "What?"

Booker's voice dripped with disdain. "Well, that guy is his dad and promised Richie he'd come back for him. Richie's loyal to his dad, so he believed him."

"That's correct," the old man affirmed. "That's why we confronted him earlier."

"Poor Richie. And Patrick, Richie's dad, just left with the rest of his goons," Nurse Dianna lamented, her heart heavy with sorrow.

The old man's voice cracked with emotion. "Dianna, I'm begging you, please save him! Richie has got to get better!"

Booker's plea was urgent. "If you don't do it soon, he won't be around for much longer. Please!"

Nurse Burke, sensing the tension, interjected softly. "Sir, we get it. Just let her help Richie."

Nurse Dianna nodded solemnly. "I'll do whatever I can."

As the scene shifted to the waiting room, the air was thick with anticipation and dread.

"All we can do now is wait," the old man murmured, his voice barely above a whisper.

"Do you think Richie's going to be alright?" Booker's voice was laced with uncertainty.

"He has to," the old man replied with conviction. "And whether or not the little guy makes it, I'm gonna make sure Patrick pays for nearly killing, no, for nearly murdering his own son!"

"That heartless monster is going to regret what he did to his son!" Booker declared vehemently.

Time crawled by, each passing moment heavy with apprehension.

"Richie, you've got to hold on! Please, keep fighting," Booker silently urged, his thoughts consumed by concern for the boy lying in the hospital bed.

A police officer entered the waiting room, a beacon of hope amidst the despair.

"I just informed my superiors at Springfield PD headquarters about the case, and they sent out an APB on Patrick. Next time I see him, I'll make sure he pays the consequences for child abuse," the officer Paul vowed.

Booker's resolve hardened. "That's good. Hopefully that monster will never hurt another kid ever again."

Finally, the treatment light flickered off, and Nurse Dianna emerged from the room.

"Well, Nurse? Is Richie?" Booker's voice trembled with anticipation.

Nurse Dianna's sigh of relief spoke volumes as she delivered the news they had been desperately waiting for.

"Richie's recovering. He should be fine by morning," she announced, her words a balm to their weary souls.

The old man's heart swelled with gratitude. "That's the spirit, Rich."

As Nurse Dianna tended to Richie, Booker slipped out of the hospital, his mind already racing with plans to find a safe haven, away from the shadows this event.

Booker sat on the edge of his hospital bed, his hands clasped tightly together. Nurse Dianna stood beside him, her expression sympathetic yet firm.

"So what happens now?" Booker asked, his voice barely above a whisper.

"You Have to Leave," Nurse Dianna said with a concerning tone in her voice.

"Nurse Dianna, I don't understand why I have to leave. I can't control my powers, but I'm not dangerous," Booker pleaded, his voice tinged with frustration as Ice was freezing the bed around him.

"Booker, it's not about you being dangerous intentionally," Nurse Dianna replied gently, her hand resting on his shoulder. "Your powers—they're unpredictable. You've already frozen the pipes in the east wing twice today."

Booker lowered his gaze, knowing she was right. "But I've been doing my best, trying to keep it in check."

"I know, but you're not making progress," Nurse Dianna acknowledged. "But it's not just about you. What if you lose control again and someone gets hurt?"

Booker's shoulders slumped. "I don't want that. I just want to get better."

Nurse Dianna nodded sympathetically. "Exactly. And we can't risk anyone's safety while you're still learning to manage your abilities."

Booker clenched his fists, fighting back tears. "I don't want to leave, though. I just did a good thing and helped save that little boy."

Nurse Dianna sighed softly. "I understand, Booker. Change is hard, especially when you're facing something as challenging as this. But this is about his safety and the safety of others."

"Okay... I guess I'll go," Booker conceded reluctantly.

As he prepared for his departure, Booker couldn't shake the feeling of leaving behind yet another place that had become his sanctuary. Yet, deep down, he knew that moving on was the right decision—a step towards mastering his powers and ensuring the safety of those around him.

Chapter 6:
Frost in the Sanctuary

Booker paced back and forth outside the hospital, fists clenched, breath visible in the crisp winter air. The sting of injustice burned within him as he replayed the scene that had just unfolded. He had saved a child's life, damn it. But instead of gratitude, all he got was fear and rejection.

"They're afraid," he muttered to himself, his voice edged with frustration. "Afraid I'll hurt someone."

He recalled how the nurses had backed away when his hands began to frost over, his powers reacting to his anger. The old man he had helped had tried to intervene, but even his earnest pleas fell on deaf ears. Now, Booker was barred from entering the hospital again.

"I just wanted to help," he murmured, more to reassure himself than anything else. The boy he had saved was safe now, whisked away into the care of doctors who saw Booker as a threat rather than a savior.

He kicked at a loose stone on the ground, sending it skittering across the icy pavement. His mind raced with conflicting emotions — anger at being judged without a chance to prove himself, sadness for the child he had saved who now only saw him as a dangerous stranger.

A bitter wind swept through the deserted parking lot, carrying with it the distant sound of sirens. Booker glanced up at the hospital's cold, imposing façade. He knew he couldn't stay here. Not now, when his very presence seemed to cause fear and panic.

With a heavy sigh, he turned away from the hospital, his steps echoing in the silence of the night. His breath formed frosty clouds as he walked aimlessly through the city streets, hands thrust deep into his pockets. He had nowhere to go and no one to turn to. The weight of his powers felt heavier than ever, a constant reminder of his loneliness.

As he walked, Booker tried to push down his anger, to find a way to accept what had happened. But it gnawed at him, a deep-seated resentment that threatened to consume him whole. He had always known his powers were different, uncontrollable at times, but he had never thought they would turn people against him like this.

In the distance, the city lights flickered against the night sky, casting long shadows across the pavement. Booker's jaw tightened as he thought about the old man and the child he had saved. Had it been worth it, he wondered? To risk everything for people who would never understand him?

He stopped suddenly, his breath catching in his throat. A dark alley yawned before him, a stark contrast to the bustling city streets. Instinctively, he knew he couldn't go back to his old life, not after tonight. The hospital had made that abundantly clear.

Booker's steps echoed through the corridor of the hospital as he made his way out into the chilly evening air. But now, as he stepped out into the dimly lit streets, he was once again confronted with the harsh reality of his existence.

With a resigned nod, Booker turned into the alley, disappearing into the shadows. He didn't know where he was headed or what lay ahead, but one thing was certain — he was alone now, more alone than he had ever been before.

And as the cold night closed in around him, Booker couldn't help but feel a flicker of something deep within him. It wasn't hope, not yet. But maybe, just maybe, it was the first ember of a fire that would someday burn bright enough to thaw the icy walls around him.

His hands stuffed into the pockets of his worn-out jacket, Booker trudged along the sidewalk, his breath forming small clouds in the frigid air. He had no destination in mind, no place to call home. All he knew was that he needed help, and he had heard whispers of a sanctuary where troubled souls could find refuge.

As he walked, Booker couldn't shake the feeling of dread that clung to him like a second skin. His powers, once a source of wonder and fascination, had become a burden too heavy to bear. He had tried to control them, to contain the icy tendrils that seemed to have a mind of their own, but with each passing day, they only grew stronger, more unpredictable.

Desperation gnawed at Booker's insides as he turned a corner and found himself standing before the looming facade of St. Michael's Church. Its stone walls seemed to exude an air of solemnity, as if aware of the weight of the secrets it held within.

With a hesitant heart, Booker pushed open the heavy wooden doors and stepped into the dimly lit interior of the church. The scent of incense hung heavy in the air, mingling with the soft murmur of prayers that filled the sacred space.

Approaching the altar, Booker spotted the figure of a man, clad in a simple robe, kneeling in prayer. He cleared his throat nervously, drawing the Reverend's attention.

The Reverend, a middle-aged man with kind eyes and a weary expression, rose to his feet and regarded Booker with a mixture of curiosity and concern. "Can I help you, my child?" he asked, his voice gentle yet tinged with authority.

Booker took a deep breath, steeling himself for what he was about to reveal. "I... I need help," he began, his voice barely above a whisper. "I'm homeless, and... and I can't control my powers."

The Reverend's brows furrowed in concern as he studied Booker intently. "Powers?" he repeated, his tone laced with disbelief.

Booker nodded, his gaze falling to the floor. "I can... I can manipulate ice," he confessed, his voice barely audible. "But I don't know how to control it. It's... it's destroying everything around me."

For a moment, there was silence as the Reverend processed Booker's words. Then, with a heavy sigh, he spoke. "I'm sorry, my child, but I'm afraid there's nothing I can do to help you."

Booker's heart sank like a stone as the weight of the Reverend's words settled upon him. "But... but I have nowhere else to go," he protested, his voice trembling with emotion.

The Reverend shook his head sadly, his expression filled with regret. "I understand, but the safety of our community must come first," he explained. "I cannot in good conscience offer you refuge here. You must seek help elsewhere."

Tears welled in Booker's eyes as he realized the magnitude of his predicament. Alone, homeless, and unable to control his powers, he was truly at the mercy of fate.

With a heavy heart, Booker turned and made his way out of
the church, the bitter cold of the night wrapping around
him like a shroud. As he disappeared into the darkness,
he couldn't help but wonder if he would ever find the
help he so desperately needed.

In the heart of the community center, Deon found himself
engulfed in the bustling activity of gathering boxes of
supplies. His uncle and Reverend McCloud stood watch
over the operations, their solemn gazes reflecting the
weight of the task at hand. Reverend McCloud's voice
cut through the air, a beacon of guidance amidst the
chaos, as he explained the profound impact these
provisions had on the lives of the homeless, especially
during the harshness of the season.

But amidst the clamor, Deon's thoughts strayed to a different
event—a party he was already late for. With a sudden
realization, he dashed out, leaving behind the mission of
charity for the allure of celebration. However, fate had
other plans in store. A call from his grandfather shattered
the anticipation, revealing a city paralyzed by snow and
ice.

The urgency in his grandfather's voice echoed in Deon's ears
as he raced through the frozen streets, his mind fixated

on one person—Booker. Confrontation became inevitable as Deon demanded Booker's presence. Yet, in the heat of the moment, it was Booker standing before him. Booker's powers erupted, casting Deon aside with a forceful blast before fleeing into the wintry night, effortlessly navigating the treacherous terrain.

Undeterred, Deon emerged from the snow-laden aftermath, his determination unyielding. Tracing Booker's elusive trail led him to a shelter, teeming with the destitute. Amidst the clutter, a torn photograph caught his eye—a poignant relic of a past life, a father and son frozen in time.

Driven by a thirst for answers, Deon sought solace in the familiarity of Booker's home, only to encounter Bookers father, Todd. Deon challenged him on his assumptions of Homophobia. Hostility hung thick in the air, but Deon refused to be swayed, challenging Todd's preconceptions with unwavering resolve. In the ensuing exchange, revelations surfaced—truths veiled by shadows of rejection and abandonment. Booker's descent into homelessness, his icy abilities consuming him, all traced back to a rift that tore a family asunder.

Seeking counsel, Deon turned to Reverend McCloud, grappling with the complexity of Booker's plight. In the hallowed confines of the church, amidst flickering candlelight, words of wisdom unfurled. He found Reverend McCloud, his gentle presence immediately calming Deon's nerves. With a deep breath, Deon approached the reverend, ready to share his concerns about Booker.

"Reverend McCloud," Deon began, his voice wavering slightly, "I need to talk to you about Booker."

The reverend regarded Deon with a compassionate gaze, inviting him to speak his mind. "Of course, Deon. Please, have a seat. What's troubling you about Booker?"

As Deon poured out his worries about his friend, he couldn't help but feel a sense of relief wash over him. Reverend McCloud listened attentively, nodding understandingly as Deon spoke.

When Deon finally finished, he looked to the reverend, his eyes pleading for guidance. "Reverend, I want to help Booker, but I'm not sure how. What should I do?"

Reverend McCloud smiled softly, his wisdom shining through. "Deon, it's important to remember that Booker is not simply a member of a group labeled 'gay people.' He is a human being, just like you and me. What he needs most is not to be categorized or treated differently, but to be understood and supported as an individual."

Deon nodded, taking in the reverend's words. "So, how can I help him then?"

The reverend placed a comforting hand on Deon's shoulder. "By being there for him, just as you would for any friend in need. Offer him your love, your support, and your understanding. Show him that he is valued for who he is, without judgment or prejudice."

Deon felt a weight lift off his shoulders as he absorbed the reverend's advice. With renewed determination, he thanked the reverend and left the church, ready to be the friend that Booker needed, no matter what challenges they might face together.

Chapter 7:
Flames of Friendship

Deon stepped out of the church, his mind a tempest of questions swirling around his friend Booker. As the snow continued to fall outside, Deon found himself standing at a crossroads, torn between the duty to his community and the bonds of family. The air was charged with tension as he navigated through the bustling streets. Yet, amidst the chill of uncertainty, one truth remained steadfast—each step forward was a testament to the resilience of the human spirit, thawing even the coldest of hearts. Little did he know that the next time they crossed paths, it would be Booker seeking him out.

"So, you're here to take me down too? Well, how about it? It's about time I get to test these powers to their full potential," Booker's voice sliced through the air, laden with challenge.

Deon's pleas fell on deaf ears as Booker's determination seemed unyielding. "This isn't the time, Booker. You need to listen to me…"

"I'm done listening to people. You'll fight me, Deon, unless of course you want the frozen Earth on your conscience," Booker interrupted, his tone laced with a bitter resolve.

Deon's heart sank. "Booker, we've been friends for years. Certainly, you wouldn't..."

But before he could finish, Deon's gaze fell upon Booker's lifted hand, and in an instant, an entire building was encased in ice. Fear gripped Deon's heart as he screamed in terror.

"Do you want to fight me because your mad at me or because you have hate in your heart?" Deon's voice wavered with uncertainty, struggling to understand the depths of Booker's rage.

Their confrontation escalated, each word a shard of ice in the growing storm between them.

"This fight is meaningless. You have people in your life who support you," Deon pleaded desperately.

"Meaningless, huh? What do you know of meaningless? You spent most of your life in a loving home. I got kicked out for being different. What has more meaning than family?" Booker's voice cracked with bitterness, his pain laid bare for the world to see.

As they squared off, the weight of their shared history hung heavy in the air, each moment a testament to the rift that had formed between them.

"I'll trust you have no more excuses?" Booker's words were a challenge, daring Deon to stand his ground.

"None... I guess I've been keeping you waiting for a long time, Booker, but no more. I'm ready now," Deon declared, steeling himself for the battle ahead.

"The table has been set. Now let us begin," Booker proclaimed, his voice echoing with finality.

With powers ablaze and ice swirling around him, Deon and
Booker clashed, each blow resonating with the weight of
their fractured bond.

"You're not going to win, not this time," Deon asserted as
flames engulfed him, melting through Booker's icy
onslaught.

"I don't know why I'm surprised." Deon muttered to himself,
his breath forming clouds in the frigid air.

But Booker's mastery over ice proved formidable as he
ensnared Deon in chains of frost, his movements
calculated and precise.

"What's the matter? Not winning as easy as you thought?"
Booker taunted, his words dripping with disdain.

As Deon struggled against his icy restraints, a fire ignited
within him, fueled by a simmering rage.

"What a clown! Are you feeling angry? Humiliated? Is that
it?" Booker's mockery only served to stoke the flames of

Deon's fury. "Fool," he spat, his words laced with bitter disdain. "You have yet to taste the true bitterness of humiliation. But fear not, for I shall be your teacher in this cruel lesson, just as my father was mine. I refuse to linger in the shadow of your superiority any longer. No more shall I be your mere 'Token.' That era has drawn to its close. With every labored breath you take, you defile the honor that is rightfully mine."

His anger palpable, Booker forged chains of frost with his frigid power, binding Deon further and forcing him to his knees. In that moment, beneath the weight of icy shackles and the venomous words of his adversary, Deon knew the true meaning of humiliation. Booker stood before him, his eyes reflecting a tumult of emotions, from anger to sorrow.

"Booker, listen to me!" Deon called out over the howling storm. "I'm not here to fight you. I want to help you."

But Booker's icy demeanor remained unchanged, his frosty barriers seeming impenetrable. Deon knew he had to try a different approach. Drawing upon his own empathy and understanding, he reached out to Booker, not with fists, but with words of compassion.

"Booker, I know you're hurting," Deon said softly, his voice cutting through the icy silence. "But you don't have to face this alone. I'm here for you, always."

Amidst the chaos of the battle, there was a moment of respite where the weight of their emotions could no longer be ignored. In a quiet corner away from the fray, Booker and Deon had a heart-to-heart conversation that would change the course of their relationship.

Booker's voice was raw with emotion as he spoke. "Do you even remember what it was like before all of this? When we were just friends, and everything was simple?"

Deon's eyes were filled with a mixture of regret and understanding. "I remember, Booker. But everything changed so quickly when I got these powers. I didn't want to leave you behind."

Booker shook his head, his frustration evident. "But that's exactly what happened. I'm just a shadow in your world now. I can't compete with the Eternal Flame."

Deon's expression softened, and he reached out to his friend. "It wasn't supposed to be this way. I never wanted you to feel left out. I've been so caught up in my own struggles that I forgot how much I needed you."

For a moment, Booker seemed to waver, his icy armor cracking ever so slightly. And then, with a heavy sigh, he lowered his guard, allowing Deon to approach.

"I thought these powers would make everything better," Booker confessed, his voice tinged with bitterness. "But they only made me feel more isolated. Like some kind of freak."

Deon's heart ached at Booker's words, the pain in his friend's eyes mirroring his own struggles. "I understand, Booker," he said gently, reaching out to him. "I may not know exactly what you're going through, but I know what it's like to feel alone, to feel like you don't belong."

Tears welled up in Booker's eyes, his icy facade melting away to reveal the vulnerable soul beneath. "I just want to be accepted for who I am," he whispered, his voice barely audible over the howling wind.

Deon wrapped his arms around Booker, offering him the comfort and warmth he so desperately needed. And to his surprise, Booker hugged him back, his icy exterior thawing under the warmth of Deon's embrace.

Together, they faced the storm, their friendship stronger than ever before. And as they emerged from the icy fortress, hand in hand, Deon knew that they would face whatever challenges lay ahead, together.

The heart-to-heart conversation was a turning point in their relationship. The raw honesty and vulnerability shared during that moment allowed both Booker and Deon to see each other's perspectives more clearly. The rebuilding of their bond was a gradual process, marked by mutual understanding and renewed commitment to their friendship.

Booker began to find his own path, embracing his unique strengths and talents. Deon, in turn, made an effort to balance his superhero responsibilities with his personal relationships. The moments they shared, though different from the past, were now infused with a deeper appreciation for each other.

As time went on, Booker and Deon's friendship evolved into a new dynamic, one that reflected their growth and the challenges they had overcome. Their renewed connection was a testament to the resilience of their bond, forged in the crucible of adversity.

Booker and Deon stood side by side, facing the horizon with a sense of hope and optimism as the ice melted around the city. Their friendship, though tested, had emerged stronger and more enduring. The flame of their connection burned brightly, illuminating their path as they moved forward into an uncertain future.

With Booker now by his side, Deon returned home, where his family welcomed them both with open arms. His grandfather, Aunt, and Uncle embraced Booker as one of the family, and showering him with love and acceptance.

As Christmas approached, Booker found himself seated with his newfound family, listening to Reverend McCloud's interfaith service on the TV. And as the reverend spoke of love, compassion, and the true meaning of Christmas, Booker realized that it wasn't about the presents or the decorations—it was about the people you shared it with, the ones who accepted you for who you were, no matter what.

And as he looked around at his family, old and new, Booker knew that he was exactly where he was meant to be—surrounded by love, acceptance, and the warmth of friendship that would never fade away.

www.ingramcontent.com/pod-product-compliance
Lightning Source LLC
Chambersburg PA
CBHW021745150726
47989CB00004B/1517